WARRIOR SON OF A WARRIOR SON

Samburumburi saandetwa?
Ol-kila loo-'musetani.
What looks like a butterfly?
The beaded cloak of a Masai girl.
                    A Masai riddle

For Cody and Max
　　　　—M. L.

For Howling Frog
　　　　—C. R.

Warrior Son of a Warrior Son is based on "The Caterpillar and the Wild Animals," from *The Masai: Their Language and Folklore,* by A. C. Hollis. Oxford: Clarendon Press, 1905.

This story is from the Masai of East Africa.

ILLUSTRATIONS © Charles Reasoner

Library of Congress Cataloging-in-Publication Data

Lilly, Melinda.
　Warrior son of a warrior son: [a Masai tale] / retold by Melinda Lilly;　illustrated by Charles Reasoner.
　　p.　cm. — (African tales and myths)
　Summary: A Masai folktale about how the tiny caterpillar outsmarts the other animals even though they are much bigger and stronger.
　ISBN 1-57103-246-0
　[1. Masai (African people)—Folklore. 2. Folklore—Africa, East.]　I. Reasoner, Charles, ill. II. Title III. Series: Lilly, Melinda. African tales and myths.
PZ8.1.L468War 1998
[398.2'089'965]—dc21　　　　　　　　　　　　　　　　　　98–23124
　　　　　　　　　　　　　　　　　　　　　　　　　　　　　　　CIP
　　　　　　　　　　　　　　　　　　　　　　　　　　　　　　　AC

Printed in the USA

WARRIOR SON

OF A WARRIOR SON

A Masai Tale

Retold by
Melinda Lilly

Illustrated by
Charles Reasoner

The Rourke Press, Inc.
Vero Beach, Florida 32964

Penina sat with her grandmother by the fire and watched the cattle lie down to sleep as night spread across the grasslands. "Kokoo, my grandmother," sighed Penina. "I've seen many seasons, but everyone still says I'm too little to help with the cattle. Will I ever be big enough to do anything?"

"Child, I don't believe I've told you about tiny Kurto the Caterpillar, whose heart was as big as his body was small. He could do nearly anything because he believed he could. Let me tell you Kurto's story," said Grandmother:

5

Netii apaa, a long time ago, Gitojo Rabbit was awakened early by the sounds of Kurto Caterpillar building a home for himself. Kurto slapped mud on the outside walls of his hut—*whap! whap!* Then he scraped the mud until the wall was smooth—*scriiitch*. For the third morning in a row, there was no sleep to be had by Gitojo.

Gitojo Rabbit huddled under the fire thorn shrub where he'd slept and watched bleary-eyed as Kurto Caterpillar worked. What a nice hut Kurto was making! Gitojo was envious. He was tired of sleeping under bushes and waking with a crick in his neck. He wanted a proper home. Actually, he wanted Caterpillar's home.

Kurto Caterpillar crawled around his finished hut. "Fine enough for the warrior I'll be someday," he congratulated himself. He turned the corner and came upon Gitojo Rabbit leaning on the doorjamb in the mouth of the hut.

"Nice place, Brother Kurto," Rabbit commented. "Nice for a hovel, that is. I thought you wanted to be murrani, a proud warrior. Isn't this place too humble?"

"One day they'll sing of the magnificence of Kurto the Warrior and his mighty home," responded Kurto. He led Gitojo on a tour. "These walls are like a warrior's shield. The roof is as strong as the roof of Sky God's palace." He ushered Rabbit inside. "The sun could sit in this fireplace!"

"Not bad," admitted Rabbit. "But if you're going to become a warrior, you'll need a big home like mine, where gold sparkles on the floor and beads shine in the ceiling." He scratched his chin, deep in thought. "Maybe I could help you out. Make a trade. Gold and beads are too fancy for me, but this shanty would suit me okay."

"Gold and beads!" said Kurto breathlessly. "How beautiful! That would better suit a warrior. . . . Yes, let's trade."

"Done," said Rabbit.

"Show me my new home, Gitojo," urged Caterpillar. He followed Rabbit through a cluster of fire thorn to the top of a nearby hill.

"Here is your home," chuckled Rabbit, gesturing at the grasslands. He scuffed the golden grass sprouting from the dirt. "This is the gold on the floor. Tonight you'll see beads sparkling in the ceiling. More than you can count."

Stunned by his bad trade, Kurto watched as Rabbit eagerly moved into his new hut. He stared as Rabbit caressed the smooth outside walls that Kurto had finished only that morning. When Rabbit disappeared inside, Kurto smelled the cozy scent of a fire burning in the wonderful hearth. He heard each snore of Rabbit's nap, knowing that Gitojo was comfortable in the soft bed that Caterpillar had made for himself!

Unable to stay away, he slumped by the doorway, wondering how he could transform himself into a warrior when he had no hut, no warrior's strength, or cleverness. All he had was a warrior's heart in a tiny caterpillar's body.

Early the next morning, Rabbit awakened and hurried out. "Make way, little one," he barked. "I'm thirsty and Frog owes me a gourd of water!" Kurto quickly moved aside.

Rabbit returned a little while later, carrying the water gourd that he'd collected from a bet with Frog. As he neared the mouth of the hut, a low voice snarled at him from inside the house. "Give me your water!"

12

Gitojo stepped back. No one was supposed to be in his new hut. He tried to see inside, but saw only blackness. "If you want water, you'll have to come out," he commanded, dangling the gourd in the dark doorway.

The deep voice hissed,

> I am mightier than War Bird.
> I am more beautiful than Leopard the Huntress.
> I look down on Lengaina Elephant.
> I am a Warrior Son of a Warrior Son!
> I'm not leaving, little one!

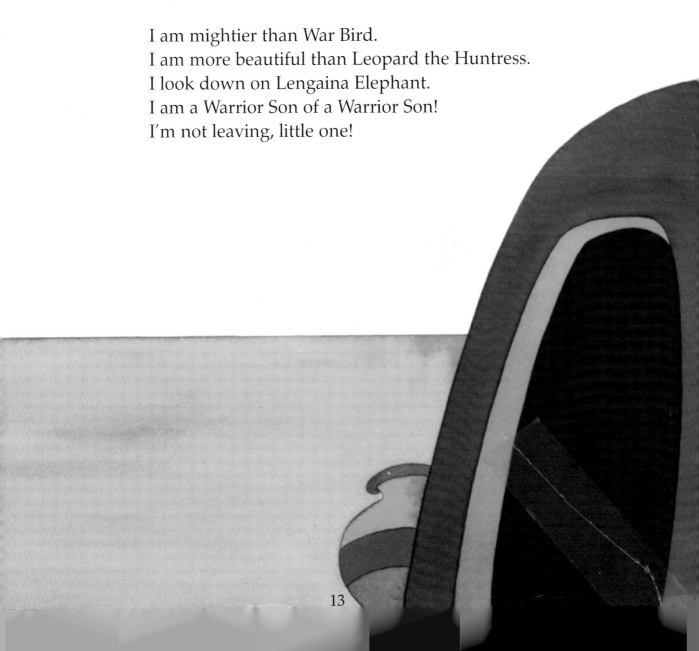

Rabbit clutched his gourd, recoiling at the frightening sound of the voice. Then he straightened up. No matter how he was threatened, Gitojo wouldn't give up his precious home! He looked around for help, spotting Kilili Eagle the War Bird and Tuaa Frog at the nearby baobab tree. Perhaps fierce War Bird could scare Warrior Son away, but Rabbit knew that he would never willingly help.

"Kilili Eagle, my neighbor," Gitojo said, casually strolling over. "A great warrior's in my hut. I think he wants to talk with you. He mentioned your name."

"He did?" said Eagle, preening. "We'll see about that." He soared above Rabbit and landed gracefully in front of the hut.

"Kilili Eagle the War Bird here," he announced. He stood tall and balanced himself on one leg in the manner of a proud Masai. "Come out and talk the talk of warriors."

A thundering voice responded:

> I am mightier than War Bird.
> I am more beautiful than Leopard the Huntress.
> I look down on Lengaina Elephant.
> I am a Warrior Son of a Warrior Son!
> I'm not leaving, little one!

Eagle backed up, wide-eyed. He hastily flew to the top of the baobab tree. "He doesn't want to talk with me," he sputtered.

"I guess I'd better find a braver animal to help me," said Rabbit as he set off across the grasslands.

Next morning, the sun rose on the silent hut and the baobab tree, where Rabbit was trying to convince Keri Leopard to help him. "Keri Leopard, you are the most beautiful huntress," he murmured as Eagle and Frog listened in. "But did you know there's a warrior son in my hut who claims he's more beautiful than you?"

"He does?" snarled Keri. Throwing off her robe and baring her teeth, she sauntered to the mouth of the hut. "Come out Warrior Son, before I come in!" she growled. "Let's see how beautiful you are now!"

I am mightier than War Bird.
I am more beautiful than Leopard the Huntress.
I look down on Lengaina Elephant.
I am a Warrior Son of a Warrior Son!
I'm not leaving, little one!

The voice rumbled and the ground shook. Leopard ran away so fast she almost left her spots behind.

Grumbling, Rabbit set off to search for a mightier animal. Someone had to be tough enough to get that terrible Warrior Son out of his new hut!

Early the next morning, Leopard, Eagle, and Frog made room for Elephant and Rabbit in the long shadows of the baobab tree. "Lengaina Elephant, if you'll get Warrior Son out of my hut, I'll give you as much grass as I gave Eagle and Leopard," said Rabbit, taking a sip from his water gourd.

Leopard narrowed her eyes to slits. "He didn't give us any food," she whispered to Eagle.

"Sounds good to me," agreed Lengaina. It was almost too easy for Rabbit to fool Elephant. Lengaina was bigger than big, but his thoughts were smaller than small.

"Well, go on, get that Warrior Son!" urged Rabbit.

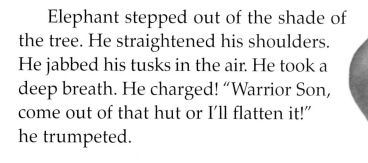

Elephant stepped out of the shade of the tree. He straightened his shoulders. He jabbed his tusks in the air. He took a deep breath. He charged! "Warrior Son, come out of that hut or I'll flatten it!" he trumpeted.

> I am mightier than War Bird.
> I am more beautiful than
>   Leopard the Huntress.
> I look down on Lengaina Elephant.
> I am a Warrior Son of a Warrior Son!
> I'm not leaving, little one!

The voice was a punishing wind, flattening the grasslands and stopping Elephant in his mighty tracks.

Lengaina Elephant hastily retreated. "He's the warrior who threw Elephant to the sky and beat Lion with his own tail!" he wailed.

t's worse than that, he's the warrior bird who swallows the grasslands in one gulp!" whimpered Eagle.

"No, he's the hungry spirit, come to crush us between his gnashing teeth!" Leopard shuddered.

Rabbit frantically scanned the plains, searching for help without success. "We're doomed!" he cried. He laid the water gourd at the mouth of the hut, then threw himself on the ground, shaking. "Warrior Son, you're mightier than all of us. I am only a little rabbit. Take my water, take my house, just let me live!" he groveled.

As he had for days, Tuaa Frog listened quietly to Rabbit's desperate pleas. He had a plan. "Brother Trickster," he whispered as he hopped over and crouched next to the prostrate Rabbit. "Calm down. I'll get Warrior Son out of there. All I ask is for you to give me back the water gourd you took from me."

"If you can get Warrior Son out of my hut, I'll not only give the gourd back, I'll haul water for you from now until the rainy season. But if Kilili with his big beak, Keri with her sharp teeth, and gigantic Lengaina with his jabbing tusks couldn't get Warrior Son to leave, how could you?" scoffed Rabbit.

"Never mind how," said Frog. "Do we have a deal?"

"Yes, anything," whined Rabbit, sitting up.

Frog approached the hut and stood by the side of the doorway. He breathed in and out, each time puffing his cheeks a little wider. When his cheeks were as large and round as a mala gourd, he spoke with an ear-splitting croak. "WARRIOR SON, COME OUT AND GREET US!"

23

24

The voice boomed like the pounding of an o-lulu drum, answering:

> I am mightier than War Bird.
> I am more beautiful than Leopard the Huntress.
> I look down on Lengaina Elephant.
> I am a Warrior Son of a Warrior Son!
> WHO CHALLENGES ME?

Now Frog breathed in and in. He gulped air until his cheeks were as huge as the sun.

> I AM THE SON OF THE WATER!
> MY MOUTH IS AS BIG AS A LAKE!
> WHEN I SPEAK, THE WAVES CRASH!
> I SAID, COME OUT AND GREET US!

The air cracked as Frog's voice traveled across the grasslands and over the mountains to the far ocean and back again. The waves of sound split the sky before finally receding into silence.

Gitojo and his neighbors quivered as they stared at the darkness in the hut. Something stared back. Something with round red eyes! From out of the mouth of the hut came Warrior Son . . .

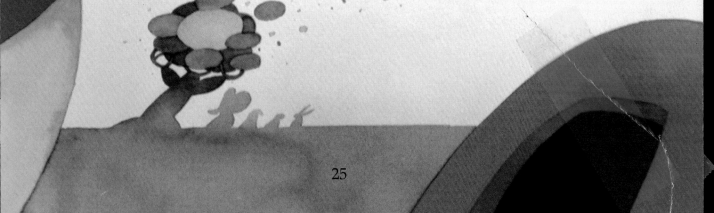

. . . a beautiful, spotted butterfly!

"You can have the hut now, Gitojo," said Kurto the Butterfly as he danced in the air. "I don't need it anymore."

"You're the warrior son of the warrior son? You're the one who was the little worm! I can't believe it!" chuckled Rabbit. He admired the sunshine glinting off Kurto's graceful wings. "Now you are a proud warrior."

"A war bird," added Eagle.

"As beautiful as I," purred Leopard.

"Of course you can look down on me!" grinned Elephant, watching Kurto flutter above his head.

"What you said about yourself was true, Warrior Son," smiled Frog. He winked at Kurto and took a long drink from the gourd he'd won back from Rabbit. He drained the last drop.

"Gitojo," he said. "I'm mighty thirsty after all this shouting. Go to the river and fetch me a full gourd of water." For many days after, until the rainy season arrived, Rabbit hauled water for little Tuaa the Frog.

Grandmother patted Penina's knee, saying, "Epwo 'mbaa pokin ingitiñgot—Everything comes to an end, even this story."

"Kokoo," Penina asked her grandmother. "How did that worm have such a big voice?"

"Maybe you've seen Kurto crossing the grasslands as part of an endless army. He and his kind are known as warrior worms, " explained Grandmother. "He had a warrior's voice and beauty, and most of all, a warrior's cleverness and heart. Like someone else I know who thinks she's too little."

PRONUNCIATION AND DEFINITION GUIDE:

gitojo (gee TOH joh): Maa (the Masai language) for rabbit.

gourd (GORD): A vine with hard fruits that can be hollowed and used as containers.

keri (KUR ee): Maa for leopard.

kilili (kee LEE lee): Maa for eagle.

kokoo (Koh KOO): Maa for grandmother.

kurto (KUR toh): Maa for caterpillar.

lengaina (len GUY nah): Maa for elephant.

mala (MAH lah): Maa for a large gourd.

maa (MAH): The language of the Masai.

Masai (Mah SIGH): A culture of East Africa.

mouth of the hut: Translation of the Maa word kutukaji. A doorway or door.

murrani (mu RAH nee): A Masai warrior.

netii apaa (neh TEE ah PAY): Maa phrase meaning "long ago." It is traditionally spoken at the beginning of a story.

o-lulu (O LOO´ loo): A large East African drum.

Penina (Peh NEE nah): A Masai girl's name

tuaa (too AY): Maa for frog.